Bank Street

ABOUT THE BANK STREET READY-TO-READ SERIES

More than seventy-five years of educational research, innovative teaching, and quality publishing have earned The Bank Street College of Education its reputation as America's most trusted name in early childhood education.

Because no two children are exactly alike in their development, the Bank Street Ready-to-Read series is written on three levels to accommodate the individual stages of reading readiness of children ages three through eight.

○ *Level 1:*   GETTING READY TO READ **(Pre-K–Grade 1)**
Level 1 books are perfect for reading aloud with children who are getting ready to read or just starting to read words or phrases. These books feature large type, repetition, and simple sentences.

● *Level 2:*   READING TOGETHER **(Grades 1–3)**
These books have slightly smaller type and longer sentences. They are ideal for children beginning to read by themselves who may need help.

○ *Level 3:*   I CAN READ IT MYSELF **(Grades 2–3)**
These stories are just right for children who can read independently. They offer more complex and challenging stories and sentences.

All three levels of The Bank Street Ready-to-Read books make it easy to select the books most appropriate for your child's development and enable him or her to grow with the series step by step. The levels purposely overlap to reinforce skills and further encourage reading.

We feel that making reading fun is the single most important thing anyone can do to help children become good readers. We hope you will become part of Bank Street's long tradition of learning through sharing.

The Bank Street College of Education

To Anna and Simone
— E.W.

For Tracy Sherrit Gray
—R.M.T.

For a free color catalog describing Gareth Stevens' list of high-quality books and multimedia programs, call 1-800-542-2595 (USA) or 1-800-461-9120 (Canada). Gareth Stevens Publishing's Fax: (414) 225-0377.

Library of Congress Cataloging-in-Publication Data

Weiss, Ellen, 1949-
    My first day at camp / by Ellen Weiss; illustrated by
Rebecca McKillip Thornburgh.
        p. cm. -- (Bank Street ready-to-read)
    Summary: Anna wants to take her lucky penny to camp on the first
day because she is feeling a little afraid.
    ISBN 0-8368-2418-0 (lib. bdg.)
    [1. Camps--Fiction. 2. Luck--Fiction. 3. Fear—Fiction.]
    I. Thornburgh, Rebecca McKillip, ill. II. Title. III. Series.
PZ7.W4472My   1999
[E]--dc21   99-18570

This edition first published in 1999 by
Gareth Stevens Publishing
1555 North RiverCenter Drive, Suite 201
Milwaukee, Wisconsin 53212 USA

Printed in Mexico

1 2 3 4 5 6 7 8 9 03 02 01 00 99

Bank Street Ready-to-Read™

My First Day at Camp

by Ellen Weiss
Illustrated by Rebecca McKillip Thornburgh

A Byron Preiss Book

Gareth Stevens Publishing
MILWAUKEE

Anna's eyes popped open.
"My first day of day camp!"
"Are you excited?" asked Mom.
"Yes," said Anna. "And scared."

"Why are you scared?" asked Mom.
"I'm afraid I won't have friends,
and I'll be lonely," said Anna.
"I think you'll be fine," said Mom.

She gave Anna a big hug.
"Everyone at Camp Sunshine
will want to make friends."
"I hope so," said Anna.

Before they left for the bus,
Anna had an idea.
"I'll take my lucky penny," she said.
"The one Grandpa Joe gave me."

It was shiny and new.
It said 1999.

Anna put it in her pocket,
then got on the big red bus.
"Have a great day!" Mom waved.
Anna waved back.

8

Anna sat all by herself.
Lots of other kids
sat with friends.
But Anna didn't know anyone.

Then a girl got on the bus.
She was wearing big blue glasses.
She sat right next to Anna.
"Hi!" said the girl.
"Hi!" said Anna.

"My name is Maria," she said.
"I'm new."
"Me too," said Anna.
She wished she had sunglasses too.

Maria told Anna about
her new baby sister.
Anna told Maria about
her new baby hamsters.

When the bus got to Camp Sunshine,
a man blew a whistle.
He called out Anna's name.
"I'm here!" she yelled.

"Jane is your counselor," he said.
"Your group is called the Bluebirds."
Maria was in the Robins.
The girls waved good-bye.

The Bluebirds sat under a tree.
Jane taught them the camp song.
The yelling part was really fun
and *really* loud.

16

"Let's go swim now," said Jane.
Anna got scared.
She didn't know how to swim.

But soon she learned
to blow bubbles in the water.

Next they made monster masks.
Matt made a silly purple one.

"Boo!" he said.
"Boo to you too!" said Anna.

Jane read them a funny book
under a shady tree.
Anna got the giggles.
So did everyone else!

When it was time for lunch,
Anna found Maria.

"See my necklace?" said Maria.
"See my mask?" asked Anna.
"Boo!" They both laughed.
Anna tried Maria's sunglasses.

After lunch, the Bluebirds
took a nature hike.
The woods were cool and quiet.

Nina was Anna's buddy.
They found flowers along the trail.

At the end of the day
all the kids sang:
"Make new friends but keep the old.
One is silver and the other gold."

On the bus
Anna sat with Maria,
who let her borrow the sunglasses.
Nina sat across from them.
They sang songs all the way home.

Anna's mom said hello with a hug.
"How was your day?" Mom asked.
"Great!" said Anna.
"My lucky penny did the trick!"

Anna told her mother all about
singing and swimming,
making masks,
and making friends.

But when they got to their door—
there was Anna's penny!
She knew it was hers.
It was shiny and new.
It said 1999.

Anna had dropped it
and never even noticed.

Anna checked her pocket.
There was a hole in one corner
just the size of a penny.

"I guess I didn't need
that penny after all," she said.
"I had lots of good luck without it."

Anna gave her mom a big hug.
She put on Maria's sunglasses.
"Now I just can't wait till tomorrow!"

MORGAN AND ME

Written By:
STEPHEN COSGROVE

Illustrated By:
ROBIN JAMES

GROLIER ENTERPRISES INC.
Danbury, Connecticut

A Serendipity Book

Dedicated to Robin James and Morgan, her horse, who I hope will always live in The Land of Later . . .

Do you ever lie on your back and gaze at the sky, wishing you were something other than you are?

In a far corner of The Land of Later, there was a beautiful princess who was always dreaming of being someone other than herself. When her chores in the castle were to be done, she could be found lying on her back, dreaming of paupers, princesses and dew drops.

She would dream she was a pauper...for she was. She would dream she was a princess...for she was. And she would dream she was a dew drop, but she really wasn't a dew drop.

One day as she was watching the clouds puff and billow across the sky, her father shouted at her from the castle, "I've told you before to clean your room. Now I find you've done nothing all day but dream!"

"I'll be there in a minute," she shouted, but instead of minding her father, she decided to take a walk in the woods.

"I don't need to clean up my room right now," she thought as she walked along the path. "I'll do it...but just a little later."

She walked deeper and deeper into the forest. The trees made a beautiful canopy over her head. The moss at her feet felt like a velvet carpet.

"I should go back before I get lost. I'll go back...but just a little later." She walked on and on into the forest.

"I should find something to eat, for I am so very hungry. I'll look for food...but just a little later."

The forest became darker, and the path became twisted and gnarled. Brambles were tearing at her clothing, but the little princess knew the path must be prettier up ahead. Besides, she could always turn around and go back later. As she walked farther, the dark shadows began closing in around her.

After what had seemed hours and hours of walking, she saw a glimmer of sunlight streaking through the branches. "That must be a meadow," she said. With that, she hurried through the stickers and darkness to the sunlight ahead.

Happily she stepped into the clearing. "What a beautiful meadow!" she thought. "There are flowers growing in every corner. And the clover...just smell the clover!"

The princess was absolutely delighted. Never had she seen anything quite so beautiful. She was still hungry and she knew she had to get home. But she could always do that... just a little later.

She was having so much fun that she had run around the meadow nearly four times before she noticed a large shape leaning against a tree. She stopped and looked. Standing next to the tree was the largest unicorn she had ever seen.

The princess was a little frightened. She had always loved horses, zebras and giraffes, and a unicorn was much like a horse. Boldly she walked right up to him and asked, "Why are you standing there, Mr. Unicorn?" Then she noticed that the unicorn's beautiful pearl horn was caught in a branch of the tree.

"My name is Morgan," he said, "and if you have a moment, I will tell you my tale."

It seems that Morgan was a fun-loving and playful unicorn. Day after day he would play tag with the bumblebees in the meadow. One day as he was frisking about, trying to catch a bumblebee, one landed right on his horn. Morgan was shocked at having the bumblebee so close and he looked up to see what it was doing.

Now, we all know that if we don't watch where we're going, we'll run into something. Sure enough, Morgan ran right into the tree and stuck his horn into the branch.

Desperately the bumblebees gathered around and tried to set Morgan free. But it was to no avail. Morgan was left all alone in the shadow of the tree . . . helplessly stuck.

Morgan asked the little princess if she would free him. If she would only help, Morgan promised to be hers for all of his days.

The princess thought for a moment and said, "I'm sorry you got stuck in the tree, Morgan. I know I should help you, and I will . . . but just a little later."

Thoughtlessly the little princess played at her leisure, and when she became bored she decided that she would help Morgan. She found a very thorny rose bush and carefully broke off a branch. Gently she climbed up on Morgan's back, and using the rose branch as a saw, began to cut through the limb. At last Morgan was free.

Morgan was very grateful. Even though the little princess had taken her time, Morgan followed her obediently through the clover.

The little princess was having so much fun that she didn't see the lily pond in the middle of the meadow. Slipping on the bank, she fell headlong into the water. Coughing and sputtering, she crawled onto a lily pad and called for Morgan to help her.

Morgan tossed his mane, smiled a wise smile and said, "I'm sorry you fell into the pond, Princess. I know I should help you and I will . . . but just a little later."

"But I'll catch cold sitting on this lily pad," said the princess. "Won't you please help me now?"

Sadly the princess thought a moment. Then she remembered all the times that her father had asked her to clean her room and she had always put it off until later. She even knew how Morgan must have felt when she told him she'd help him . . . later.

With a tear in her eye and a lump in her throat, she said, "Morgan, I'm sorry for always living in the Land of Later. Please help me. I promise always to do what should be done now, instead of 'just a little later'."

Morgan nodded his head and slowly lowered his great horn so the princess could climb from the water.

Then and forever after, Morgan and the little princess were the closest of close friends.

Now, when the princess and Morgan have finished all their chores, they lie upon the grass and dream of being something other than what they are. They dream of paupers, princesses and dew drops. And sometimes...just so he won't scare anybody...Morgan doesn't wear his horn.